Pelusa

a marvelous tale

Pelusa, a Marvellous Tale
by Father Luis Coloma is a project of the
America Needs Fatima Campaign
Translation, adaptation and illustrations
by Andrea F. Phillips

First American Edition © 2008
by The American Society for the Defense of Tradition,
Family and Property (TFP)
P.O. Box 341, Hanover, Pennsylvania 17331

Library of Congress Control Number: 2008923803
ISBN-13: 978-1-877905-39-1
ISBN-10: 1-877905-39-9

Printed in the United States of America

YOUR CHILD'S LIBRARY OF INNOCENCE

To my parents who led me up
the wondrous path of our Catholic
Faith; to my six brothers and sisters –
the first audience for my stories and
companions in the journey; to my
brothers-in-law – each a matchless gift to
our family; to my nephews and nieces,
priceless new life and inspiration;
and last but certainly not least,
to my beloved husband, friend and
companion, whose support and
encouragement never flags.

Andrea

About the Author

Luis Coloma was born of a distinguished family in Jerez, Spain, in 1851. From his youth he showed signs of a brilliant intelligence and a great aptitude for literature. He studied law at the University of Seville and received his doctorate in 1874. Nevertheless, having felt a strong religious call, he entered the Society of Jesus that same year.

Among many other things, he spent his life as a Jesuit between teaching and writing.

Father Coloma holds an eminent place in Spanish literature as a novelist and biographer. A great part of his work was written in the form of short stories full of Spanish "sprite" and laden with moral meaning, which he used as an efficacious apostolic tool. In 1908 he became a member of the Spanish Royal Academy of Letters, a belated honor. He died in 1915 at the age of sixty-four.

"Pelusa," one of his many children's stories, is the tale of a little girl's journey to her rightful inheritance despite the machinations of a wicked witch—obviously a parallel of the Christian soul's journey. "Pelusa" is taken from *Obras Completas* de P. Luis Coloma (Madrid: 1960).

Pelusa

a marvelous tale

By Father Luis Coloma, S.J.
Translation, adaptation and illustrations
by Andrea F. Phillips

Part One

nce upon a time there was an old woman who was as ugly and evil as sin. She was called old woman Cobwebs. This old woman Cobwebs had a little girl who lived with her. She was about five or six years old and was as sweet and fair as an angel. The little girl was called Pelusa and everyone took it for granted that she was old Cobwebs' granddaughter, but she was really no relation at all.

When little Pelusa was a baby, old Cobwebs snuck into the gardens of a magnificent palace and kidnapped her while she slept in a flowerbed. Her nurse, who should have been watching her, was visiting with her fiancé. The gate to the garden was open, so old woman Cobwebs tiptoed in, grabbed the sleeping baby, stuffed her into a bag of rags, and ran away as fast as her crooked legs could carry her. She had planned to raise the little girl to do all the housework so she could spend a lot of time flying around on her broom and visiting all her friends. For that is what old Cobwebs really was—one of those wicked,

wicked witches who fly around the air on brooms.

The witch was a terrible miser, so she brought up little Pelusa on bread crumbs. But noticing she was so skinny, the town baker and his wife slipped her lots of goodies that kept the little girl plump and rosy. The farmer and his wife would also give her vegetables and a chicken once in a while with which Pelusa learned to make delicious soup. At first, the old woman grumbled, but as she was a very big glutton, and Pelusa was a very good cook, she stopped complaining.

Growing older, little Pelusa often wondered why other children had a father and a mother while she had none. One day, in tears, she asked the old woman:

"But grandmother, why don't I have a Papa and a Mamma like all the other children?"

"Because I found you in a rabbit's nest!" shrieked the old woman furiously, "and that is why your name is 'Pelusa' because 'pelusa' is the fur they use to build their nests! So there!"

Then, to stop her tears, old Cobwebs poked her with a big black-headed knitting needle and told her to "scoot"! Poor little Pelusa hid under a table and, crying very softly so that the old woman could not hear her, sadly whimpered:

"Oh, if only I had a Papa! If only I had a Mamma!"

2

One day old woman Cobwebs went out to mail a letter and left little Pelusa sitting on the front steps to watch a pot of soup that was cooking for lunch. While the soup simmered, Pelusa played with an old broken doll that she had found in the trash. The little thing was worn and faded and missing a leg, but since Pelusa had never had any other toy, this one looked just beautiful to her. She named the doll Angelina after a heavy-set lady who lived down the street and sold hats with plumes on them.

"Since I have neither a Papa nor a Mamma," thought little Pelusa, "I will at least have Angelina and I will be her mamma."

So she made the doll a

4

dress with some colored paper she had found in the street and a bonnet with a feather plucked from a chicken.

That day, as little Pelusa played with Angelina on the front steps of the house and kept an eye on the simmering soup, she happened to see a man and a lady with a child in her arms coming up the street. They looked very poor, and very tired—as if they had traveled a long way. When they reached the entrance to Pelusa's house, the lady sat down on the first step with the little boy; she looked exhausted. And the man, also looking very tired, leaned against the wall.

Pelusa, who had a very good heart, felt sorry for them. Running inside, she brought out two chairs and

5

kindly offered the weary travelers a seat.

"Would you care to sit down to rest?" she asked.

"God bless you, my child," said the lady as she took the chair. "We are very tired because we have walked many miles and still have far to go. Besides, we have had nothing to eat all day."

"The little boy either?" asked Pelusa, as her eyes filled with tears.

"No," said the lady.

"Oh, poor, poor child!" exclaimed Pelusa. "Well, then you shall have this soup that has just finished cooking! I'm sure the little boy will like it."

And in the twinkling of an eye, she brought out a table, spread out a white tablecloth, and placed three bowls on it. She then fetched the pot with the soup and served it most graciously.

When the little boy smelled the soup, he woke up and, sitting on his mother's knees, reached out for the warm bowl.

As they ate, the lady looked kindly at Pelusa and asked her, "Do you live here with your father and mother?"

"I never had a father and a mother," said Pelusa lowering her head in shame.

"Then how did you come into this world?" asked the man, who found this answer very strange indeed.

"Old woman Cobwebs says that she found me in a rabbit's nest. That's why I am called Pelusa."

The lady and the man exchanged glances,

and little Pelusa continued sadly:

"And that's why I have no one to love me except Angelina; she is my child and I am her mother."

As she spoke, she brought out Angelina from her pocket. As soon as the little boy saw the doll, he clapped delightedly and reached out his little hands. Pelusa gladly handed him Angelina. Taking the doll in his left hand, he traced a blessing over her with his right hand, and let her go with a flourish.

Lo and behold! A marvelous thing happened. Indeed, Pelusa's hair stood on end—but not in fear for it was impossible for the boy to be sweeter or the lady more beautiful, or the man kinder but in amazement, for this is what happened:

As soon as the little doll touched the table, she stood up like a living person all by herself. Her missing leg was back in place, her broken nose was straightened, and her faded face was now as fresh, rosy and shiny as if she had just come from the store.

And while the little boy rocked on his mother's lap and clapped his hands, Angelina skipped and danced with as much grace as an accomplished ballerina. As Christmas was approaching, she sang in a piping little voice,

"To Bethlehem I'll go
Under sun, snow or rain,
For I also wish to see
This Child sovereign."

On hearing the carol, the lady looked over to the man and smiled; and he, looking at the child in her arms, bowed his head slightly.

When the little doll had finished her song, the lady extended her hand over her, and in a single leap Angelina was back in Pelusa's pocket, peeping out from a hole in the fabric to see what would happen next.

The lady smiled affectionately at Pelusa and said:

"Little Pelusa, what old woman Cobwebs said about finding you in a rabbit's nest is a very big lie. Like all other children, you have a handsome, kind father and a beautiful, kind mother who have been looking for you ever since you were stolen from them."

When she heard this, it was all Pelusa could do to keep her feet from carrying her off that very moment to that handsome father and that kind mother. With her cheeks flushed as pink as a rose and her eyes sparkling like stars, she exclaimed:

"And where are they?!"

"In the Castle of No Return, where they are under the spell of witch Cobwebs," answered the lady in her beautiful, calm voice.

Little Pelusa began to cry at this, and sadly asked:

"But where is this castle? Who will take me there? I am too

small and can not go alone!"

"Don't worry, my Pelusa. Don't cry, my child," said the lady as she fondly stroked her hair. "Angelina will take you."

"Yes indeed, my lady," piped Angelina who was peeping out from the hole in the pocket, "it will be my pleasure to take her."

"Then, when will I see my Papa and Mamma?" asked Pelusa, beside herself with joy, hope and impatience.

"Again, when the time comes, Angelina will take you there," said the lady kindly. "Do everything she tells you, and if you are ever in trouble, say with all your heart:

"Jesus, Mary and Joseph,
    Help me and guide me!"

The lady then took the small soup pot, and blessing it, handed it to Pelusa, saying:

"Take this pot and whenever you feel hungry, fill it with clear water, throw in two or three pebbles—depending on how hungry you are—and place it on the fire. Before covering it, say:

"Little pot, boil and bake
Give me something good to eat
For that sweet child's sake."

After saying this, the lady said goodbye. She and the man each kissed Pelusa on the forehead. The little boy threw his tiny arms around her neck and, while his mother held him, gave her twelve kisses—as many as the fruits of the Holy Ghost.

*B*ut just as that honorable family disappeared down the road, who did Pelusa see coming around the corner but old woman Cobwebs, snorting and hobbling with her old stick, and looking like sour vinegar. She was muttering to herself in the foulest of moods, and her breath alone made the flies drop dead all around her.

Little Pelusa froze as she remembered that the poor travelers had eaten all of the soup and there was nothing left for old woman Cobwebs! Terrified at this thought, the poor girl ran into the house and hid under the table. Trembling with fright, she awaited the first outbreak of the old woman's fury.

In no time at all, old Cobwebs came into the house and began to yell for Pelusa:

"Pelusa! Pelusa! Where are you, you good-for-nothing girl?! Bring me the soup! I'm starving!"

The poor child curled up

even tighter under the table, not even daring to breathe. But the worst was yet to come, for just then the old witch saw the empty pot on top of the table and exclaimed in a horrible rage:

"WHO ate my soup?!"

Panic stricken, Pelusa thought that maybe she could blame it on the cat. But this was not the truth and since she was a very good girl who would not tell a lie for anything in the world, because lying is a sin against the law of God, she decided to tell the truth.

"I served it to some poor hungry travelers with a beautiful child," she ventured to whisper in a trembling voice.

Green with fury, the old woman began to strike the floor with her stick.

"So you say that the child was beautiful, eh?" she said. "A pretty child indeed! May the soup turn to poison in his stomach!"

"Oh, don't say that for God may punish you!" exclaimed Pelusa, who by this time was terribly frightened. "Look, I will make you another pot of soup right this instant!"

"So you are going to make me another pot of soup, eh?" said the witch with a wicked grin that made the poor girl's blood freeze in her veins. "O no, you are not. Come here you little brigand!"

Dragging the girl by the scruff of her blouse, she tied her to the foot of the table with a big rough rope, then declared,

"I'm going to buy me a delicious pizza and you are going to sit there and watch me eat it! And guess what? There is where you will sleep tonight!"

"O, am I in trouble!" thought Pelusa. Then, remembering what the kind lady had told her, she shut her eyes tightly and whispered with all her soul,

"Jesus, Mary and Joseph,
help me and guide me!"

Just then a thundering voice that came from Pelusa's pocket said:

"Wretch!!! Let the girl go!!!"

At the same moment, the little doll Angelina leaped like a frog onto the old woman's huge nose. Mounting it as a horse, she began to scratch it so fiercely with her tiny wooden nails that soon it was looking like a big red tomato. The old woman screamed in terror dancing around the room as she attempted to tear away the terrible "clip". But the more she tried, the harder Angelina clung, all the while shouting in her piping little voice:

"Shameless old woman, let the girl go or you will carry these "spectacles" to the day you die!"

Old Cobwebs had no other choice but to untie Pelusa. As soon as Pelusa was free, Angelina leaped onto the table, leaving the witch's huge nose looking like a glowing eggplant.

17

"Now, Pelusa, make the old woman some soup," said the doll.

And because she was as good as baked bread and had not a mean bone in her, Pelusa took the pot just as the lady had instructed, filled it halfway with water and threw in two pebbles. She placed it on the fire and, before covering it, said:

"Little pot, cook and bake
Give me something good to eat
For that sweet child's sake."

Old Cobwebs watched all this open-mouthed and wide-eyed but did not dare say a word because Angelina paced furiously up and down the table, watching her out of the corner of her eye ready to pounce back on her nose.

When the water began to boil, Pelusa raised the lid and could hardly believe her eyes. Instead of clear water and two pebbles, there were two deli-cious-looking quails stewed in a savory sauce that filled the whole kitchen with a heavenly aroma.

Soon, the fragrant smell reached the bruised nose of the old witch. Greedy

and bad mannered as she was, she snatched the pot from Pelusa, gulped down the two quails, bones and all, drank the sauce like water, and finished by loudly licking her lips and fingers. Then settling into the rocking chair, she said with a big yawn:

"Now I am going to take a nap. You, Pelusa, flick the flies away."

Little Pelusa picked up a flyswatter and stood by the witch. But it was not really necessary for the very pores of the old witch's skin were poisonous and any fly that landed on old Cobwebs paid for his foolishness with its life. Soon, the old woman began to snore like the bellowing pipes of an old rusty organ.

But, as the witch slept, Pelusa noticed that she was filling out like a big balloon; first her stomach, then her head, then her hands and feet. As Pelusa and Angelina watched riveted to the floor, the old woman slowly lifted out of her chair and flew out the window. No one could tell where old Cobwebs went, except that her shoe ended up on top of the church steeple. (And there it remains to this very day, for the church sacristan, Johnny Shivers, made a weather vane from it and placed it at the very top of the bell tower so nobody forgets what happens to evildoers).

And all this was a punishment from God because old Cobwebs had cursed the little boy who had eaten her soup: "May the soup turn into poison in his stomach!" And that, my child, is because God sees everything, and can demand payment for good or bad actions without a second's notice.

21

Part Two

fter the witch disappeared, Angelina said in her cricket-like voice:

"Pelusa, put on your blue bonnet, take the magic pot and let us be off."

"Where will we go?" asked Pelusa.

"The time has come to go and look for your father and mother."

Beside herself with joy, Pelusa put on her blue bonnet and hung the pot on her arm with a ribbon through the handle. Shutting the door behind them, she reverently said the words the good lady had taught her:

"Jesus, Mary, and Joseph, help me and guide me," and started on the road, with Angelina in the lead. They walked very fast because every moment was precious for little Pelusa, who could hardly wait to find her parents. At every big house that came into view, she asked the doll:

"Is this the Castle of No Return?"

"Not yet! Further on, further on!"

"But where is this wonderful castle that seems to be hiding from us?"

"It is a bit further, beyond the next two towns."

"And why is it called the Castle of No Return?"

"Because Mr. Thunderbolt, a bad and ugly giant who lives there, will eat anyone who dares to enter the castle."

"Well, he won't eat me because I will say what the good lady taught me: 'Jesus, Mary and Joseph, help me and guide me!'" exclaimed Pelusa, who in her joy was afraid of nothing.

Around noon, they decided to rest a little under a tree. And since joy does not hinder appetite, Pelusa felt hungry.

"I wish I could eat two fried eggs right now," thought little Pelusa to herself hungrily.

And with this thought, she filled the little pot with water from a nearby spring, threw in three pebbles, made a fire with a few dry twigs and, before covering the pot, said:

"Little pot, cook and bake
Give me something good to eat
For that sweet child's sake."

The pot boiled, Pelusa raised the lid, and there, to her delight, were two fried eggs with butter. For dessert, there were two cookies dipped in chocolate, which were Pelusa's favorite. The little girl ate everything and had just finished when she heard someone calling her from above:

"Pelusa! Pelusa!"

She looked up. On a branch of the tree she saw a small black

bird, a little bigger than a sparrow, with a green beak and red feet who asked: "Pelusa, where are you going?"

"I am on my way to find my father and my mother and my true home," answered the girl.

"Oh, there will be plenty of time to find them later," replied the black bird. "Come with me and I will take you to my friend's house, which is all made of candy and sweets. The walls are covered with cookies, the doors are made of milk chocolate, the fences and verandas are lollipops, the furniture is built of almond nougat, and the beds have marshmallow pillows. Pelusa, I know you will love this house because you love candy and sweets."

"No, little bird, no," answered Pelusa firmly.

"I am on my way to find my father and mother, and I must continue right now."

While the little bird spoke, Angelina was quietly climbing the tree, inch by inch. When she reached the branch where the bird was perched, she snuck up behind him without making a sound. Then, with a quick motion, she grabbed him by the neck and threw him to the ground below. As he flew away with a loud squawk, he left behind a terrible burnt smell. "That was one of those bad birds that the devil sends to this world to tempt good children from doing their duty," Angelina told Pelusa.

And so they continued on their way. They walked, through valleys and over mountains, eating what the little pot provided and sleeping under trees. On the third day, as they sat down to eat, the little pot was very generous: there was delicious baked chicken, French fries and a salad, and last of all, the two cookies dipped in chocolate that Pelusa liked so much and that came with every meal.

She was ready to eat them when she saw a flock of goldfinches, which had landed around her, begging for some small alms for the love of God.

Pelusa's first impulse was to give

them the cookie that she was about to put in her mouth, but then she remembered the other black bird of the devil who tried to deceive her. So she stopped—now very suspicious of little birds.

Angelina looked at her seriously and said:

"Pelusa, in this world there are many bad people but there are also many good people; true wisdom is knowing how to tell the bad ones from the good ones. That other little bird was bad because he was a bird of the devil and wanted to distract you from your journey home. But these little birds belong to God and they are so good that they once mourned Jesus' death on Mount Calvary. That is why their song says:

"On top of Mount Calvary,
Where Christ hung dead and pale,
Mourning their God pityingly,
Were four goldfinches and a nightingale."

Pelusa smiled happily as she gave the little finches not only one but both of the cookies that she was about to eat. As they pecked away, happy with their meal, they sang for Pelusa one of those beautiful symphonies that God taught birds to sing.

And so Pelusa and Angelina continued on their way. At
sunset of that day, they were only a short distance from
the Castle of No Return! It was a very big, brown build-
ing with only a small door and no windows. The sight of
such a dark, mysterious place sent a chill down their backs.

With no little fear, Pelusa and Angelina approached. The doll
stepped forward to knock on the door, but Pelusa stopped her.
Kneeling down on the cold steps, she fervently prayed:

"Jesus, Mary, and Joseph,
help us and guide us."

Then, with renewed courage, Angelina boldly knocked.

There was a muffled noise, then the sound of falling chains as the door opened to reveal an elegant owl with golden spectacles. The owl wore a black dress and a complicated hat with orange bows. She held out a lantern with a green shade, and politely asked:

"What can I do for you?"

As she was so elegant, Angelina asked if she was Mr. Thunderbolt's wife.

"No, Madam," answered the owl. "I am his housekeeper Brumhilda."

"My lady, would it be possible for us to see Mr. Thunderbolt?" asked Angelina respectfully.

"That would be quite difficult," replied the owl. "The poor thing spent the whole night groaning and moaning with a toothache and he is now resting."

Hearing this, Angelina lifted the palm of her hand to her forehead in astonishment, and exclaimed:

"But this is providential, my Lady Brumhilda! Tell the giant that he happens to have at his very doorstep, Dr. Angelina, famous dentist who can cure any toothache!"

29

"But really?!" exclaimed the owl in delight. "Oh, step in, step in. I will go and tell him right away. How happy the poor thing will be!"

The housekeeper ushered them into a square room all draped in black, and left them there, turning the key on the lock as she left. Little Pelusa was afraid because she thought that the owl had tricked them and had locked them in the dark room as prisoners. After a long, lonely wait, they heard a terrifying sound of dragging chains. Then, a sad voice groaned from above:

"Should I fall or should I not?"

Three times the voice repeated the question.

Pelusa did not dare to answer, but Angelina, who in her nervousness was growing irritable, finally called out angrily at the top of her voice: "Come down then!"

The ceiling opened and a leg fell to the ground. But it was not just an ordinary leg. O, no! It was an enormous leg with a red silk stocking and a large yellow leather shoe.

A long silence followed. Then, again, they heard the same sound of dragging chains, and that same eerie voice, "Should I fall or should I not?"

By now Angelina had no more patience and answered furiously: "Will you just fall once and for all?!"

The ceiling opened again and another leg fell; it was the perfect match of the other except that it had a red shoe and a yellow stocking.

Four times they heard the same dragging chains and the same

moaning voice ask:

"Should I fall or should I not?"

And one after the other fell, first one arm, then another, then the trunk of a body and then finally a huge head with a red beard. A large black bandanna was tied around the head to ease the pain of the toothache.

Then in one sweep, all the pieces, legs, arms, trunk, and head—joined together to make the body of Mr. Thunderbolt, who would not have been so bad looking but for his horrible swollen jaws. He had a huge mustache that curled at the tips and reached all the way to his eyes. He looked sad and upset, and as he seated himself on a huge chair, began to complain and to tug at his flaming beard,

"Oh, my tooth! Oh, my tooth! Oh, my tooth!"

Little Pelusa and Angelina had taken shelter in a corner of the room, but after this character had collected himself and sat down, Angelina majestically crossed the room and leaped up onto the table in order to be closer to the giant's ear. With all the eloquence of a famous dentist, she proclaimed:

"Now, calm yourself, Mr. Thunderbolt, for there is healing for every ill, and you are fortunate enough to have before you Dr. Angelina, famous dentist, who will fix your toothache in no time at all!"

Quite surprised, the giant reached down and picked up the little doll by her head and placed her on the palm of his hand.

"Are you the Dr. Angelina that my housekeeper Brumhilda announced?"

"At your service," said the doll, parading on the giant's hand with as much pomp as if she were walking down Main Street. "I am Dr. Angelina, dentist practicing in the capital. I first practiced in the Newland District. But the other dentists there became extremely envious of me because all the patients came my way. So then I opened my own office on the east side of the city where the Duke of Snowpeaks, who is a very good friend of mine, lent me an apartment free of charge, so much does he value my work. My patients include the highest nobility in the court. Why, just the other day, I pulled three teeth

from the King's royal mouth while he was asleep, and he didn't even feel it. I clean Her Majesty's teeth twice a week and I pulled a molar—roots and all—from the mouth of the Minister of War. You should have seen those roots! They reached all the way down to his ankles! And have you heard about His Excellency the Bishop? He had not a single tooth left in his most illustrious mouth. Well, I gave him a little medicine of mine and by the time evening had set in, he had a new set of teeth as fine as that of a young boy!"

The giant opened his eyes very wide and interrupted Angelina, asking her anxiously:

"And can you fix my tooth also?"

"But of course I can! Why shouldn't I? Open your mouth just a little and let me look to make sure I don't pull out the wrong molar."

The big fool opened his mouth as wide as a cave. Holding on to the hairs of the giant's beard, Angelina climbed up and peeped in cautiously to examine the upper teeth. She then climbed up on his mustache to have a good view of the bottom ones.

Then, suddenly, with one single leap, she hopped inside and began to dance, skip and do somersaults in his throat. Mr. Thunderbolt choked and coughed but the brave little doll held on with all her might and went further and further down his throat. As he could not rid himself of the bothersome dentist with his coughing, he began to let out such huge puffs and snorts that the doors and even the walls trembled.

Meanwhile, the fearless little doll had succeeded in climbing all the way down. Reaching the heart of that bad giant, she took out a little bottle from her pocket and sprayed a mysterious anesthetic all around it. Then, as quickly as her skinny arms could haul her, she climbed up his throat again. When she finally came out, the giant let out a terrible snort, stretched out one leg and then the other, made a horrible face and finally lay there snoring up a storm. Dr. Angelina had sent Mr. Thunderbolt into a long, long sleep.

Then a tremendous sound of thunder echoed through the rooms, and the castle collapsed. But, strangely enough, not a stone struck the ground. Instead they were all carried away by a legion of small, hideous creatures who flew away with them and disappeared in the distance. These creatures were of every color except white. Some were yellow, some blue, some red, and a good number of them were green.

As the castle disappeared, Pelusa and Angelina found themselves standing before a very tall wall made of pure crystal which enclosed a beautiful garden. Looking through the crystal, they could see magnificent flowerbeds and bushes, water fountains that shot up high in the air, and long pathways flanked by tall trees.

*W*alking down one of these paths was a beautiful lady on the arm of a noble knight. She wore a beautiful pink gown trimmed in ermine. Her hair shone like sunbeams. The knight had a golden mustache, a handsome coat embroidered in gold, and an elegant hat with a peacock feather.

Nevertheless, they seemed very sad and downcast, and the lady said with tears in her eyes:

"Oh, my little girl, I wonder where she is now!"

"Don't cry, my dear wife," replied the man to comfort her. "Perhaps she will come today." But he was really just as sad as she was.

Pelusa knew right away that this knight and this lady were her very own parents. Overcome with happiness, she began to knock on the crystal wall, shouting:

"Papa! Mamma! Here I am!"

But the couple could not hear her voice through the crystal wall, for they were still under a spell. So Pelusa and Angelina walked all around the wall trying to find either a door or a window. But they did not find a single opening or crack. The crystal was hard as a rock and surrounded the entire garden so that none could enter.

Then little Pelusa saw her father and mother entering a grove of orange trees, lilacs and roses. They sat down at a table covered with a beautiful damask cloth and set with exquisite china and silver-ware. There were only two places but the lady, still crying softly, said to the page:

"Bring in my daughter's chair in case she comes today."

Immediately a small chair was brought and a small silver plate and pink crystal glass were set before it. Seeing this, Pelusa vaguely remembered having eaten and drunk from that plate and goblet when she was still very small.

With her heart torn with pain, she cried pitifully: "Oh, if I were only a little bird, I could fly over this wall and give my dear mother a kiss!"

No sooner had she finished saying this than the flock of goldfinches appeared. They landed all around her and tried to console her with their merry songs. They had brought with them a large silver net with a bed of roses arranged in it. Pelusa understood. She sat in the center with Angelina. Then, carefully holding the ends of the net with their beaks, the birds flew over the wall and placed her gently right on the table just as her mother was sadly repeating:

"But where can my little girl be?"

"Here I am, Papa! Here I am, Mamma!" exclaimed Pelusa, who hopped out of the bed of roses holding the smiling and triumphant Angelina in her hand.

With that, the spell was broken, and the three hugged and kissed and spent a whole month and a half hugging and kissing while the goldfinches sang many variations on the theme:

"Joy!... Joy!... Joy!"

And now we might add that Pelusa became a charming little princess—which she always was, just that no one knew it—and Angelina remained her inseparable friend. Wherever Pelusa went, there was the little doll reminding her of her duties and giving her good advice, for she was very wise. After all, there was a lot in that Little Boy's blessing.

The End